The Great Food Feud

OR
A Little Give and Take

Brian Sibley

Illustrations by Rosslyn Moran

A LION PICTURE STORY

Once upon a time—a very long time ago—there were two towns. One was called Aralia and the other was called Zedonia. Each town stood on a hill and between the hills ran a wide river crossed by a fine old stone bridge.

Because there were no walls or gates to the towns, the people could come and go as they pleased and lived in peace and harmony with each other.

The Aralians grew fruit and vegetables while the people of Zedonia kept cows and chickens.

Every day, people from Aralia crossed the bridge to Zedonia with barrowloads of firm white potatoes, crisp green lettuces, fat brown onions and sweet red apples.

And every day, people from Zedonia crossed the bridge to Aralia with buckets of creamy milk, trays of large speckled eggs, golden butter and cheeses the size of cartwheels.

Nobody paid for anything, but everybody always had everything they needed.

One day the King of Zedonia's Chancellor thought of something he hadn't thought of before.

"Your Majesty," he asked, "why do we give the Aralians milk and cream and butter and cheese and eggs, when all we ever get from them is a few strawberries?"

"They're jolly good strawberries!" replied the King, who was having his tea at the time. "Besides, they give us a lot of other things, too—like cabbages and potatoes."

"Potatoes!" snorted the Chancellor. "Any fool can grow a few potatoes!"

Taking another strawberry, the King asked what he should do about it.

"Tell them we will not go on being exploited!" replied the Chancellor. "Demand that they double the amount of everything they give us!"

The Queen of Aralia was so worried when she got the King of Zedonia's message that she sent for her Prime Minister.

"If you give the Zedonians what they're asking for," the Prime Minister told her, "we will have to go hungry ourselves. But if they don't get what they want, they may try to take it by force! Then there would have to be a WAR!"

"Unthinkable!" said the Queen. "We've never had a war!"

"But if we *did*," said the Prime Minister, "the Zedonians could simply march across the bridge and attack us! We must *destroy* it without delay!"

"Oh, dear," sighed the Queen. "I suppose we don't have any choice, but I will miss having cream with my strawberries . . ."

That night, a hooded figure carried a large barrel of explosives down the hill from Aralia, leaving a trail of gunpowder as he went. The Prime Minister (for that is who it was) placed the barrel in the middle of the bridge, then hurried back to the town. He lit the gunpowder and put his fingers in his ears. A spark hissed and fizzed away into the darkness, and then . . .

"What was that?" asked the King of Zedonia in a terrible panic.

"It's WAR!" said the Chancellor. "Obviously the Aralians were trying to blow up the town! It's lucky they only blew up the bridge! Next time it might be our homes and shops and schools—even *the Palace!* We must defend ourselves!"

"How?" asked the King, turning rather pale.

"We must build a wall! And we must begin AT ONCE!"

"Oh, dear," sighed the King, "I suppose we don't have any choice, but I will miss having strawberries with my cream . . ."

As soon as it was morning, the Chancellor began supervising the building. Everyone had to help: carrying wheelbarrows full of sand, mixing cement, breaking rocks, digging foundations, putting up scaffolding and laying stones.

Day and night they worked, and as the wall around Zedonia grew higher and higher, the people of Aralia grew more and more worried.

"But why are they building a wall?" asked the Queen of
Aralia anxiously.

"It is obvious," replied the Prime Minister. "They are
getting ready to launch an All Out Offensive against us!"

"But we will be defenceless!" moaned the Queen.

"Not if *we* also build a wall, just like theirs—only higher
and stronger!"

So they did.

"Why are the Aralians building a wall that is even higher than ours?" demanded the King of Zedonia.

"I imagine," the Chancellor replied darkly, "it is so that they can stand on the battlements and fire things at us."

"Fire things?" squeaked the King.

"Arrows, stones, cannon-balls, the usual things . . ."

"B-B-But," stuttered the King, "we'll all be killed!"

"Not if we build our wall HIGHER!" replied the Chancellor triumphantly.

So they did.

"The Zedonians' wall is even higher than ours," said the Queen of Aralia peering over the top of her own wall.

"Not for long!" replied the Prime Minister, "I have given the order to make our wall *EVEN HIGHER!* And we'll build buttresses and ramparts and towers and turrets!"

So they did.

And that's how both towns went on, until they finally ran out of stones. But by that time, the walls were so high that no one in Zedonia could see the town of Aralia, and no one in Aralia could see the town of Zedonia.

Everyone felt safer, although sometimes the people of Aralia wished they had something to pour over their strawberries and sometimes the people of Zedonia wished they had something to dip in their cream.

Many years went by. Then, one morning, the Queen of
Aralia got something of a surprise.

"Mashed potato for breakfast!" she grimaced, angrily
pushing her plate away. "*What* is the meaning of this?"

"I'm afraid there is something of a food shortage at
present, ma'am," explained the Prime Minister.

"But we grow every type of fruit and vegetable there is!"

"Unfortunately, we are having problems with the rain."

"Nonsense!" laughed the Queen. "It hasn't rained for
months!"

"*That*, ma'am, is the problem!" the Prime Minister
explained. "There is a drought; the plants and trees are dying
and food is getting scarce. We do still have a few sacks of
potatoes, ma'am, so you won't go completely hungry—at
least, not for a week or so . . ."

"Deary me," muttered the Queen, "if only we hadn't
fallen out with Zedonia, we could have asked them for help."

"What is this supposed to be?" asked the King of Zedonia, pointing at his plate.

"Cheese, your Majesty," replied the Chancellor.

"But there's hardly enough here to put in a mouse-trap!"

"Regrettably true, your Majesty. It's due to drought, you see; the grass has dried up and the cows can't make milk. We have one or two cheeses left, but when they've gone, well . . ." his voice trailed helplessly away.

"This is terrible!" stormed the King. "What a nuisance we're not still on friendly terms with Aralia; we could have asked them to help us."

"I have a plan, ma'am," said the Prime Minister of Aralia. "We will INVADE Zedonia! And to do that, we will build a bridge!"

The Queen looked astonished. "I thought we blew up a bridge so that the Zedonians *couldn't* invade *us*, and now we are going to build a bridge so that we *can* invade *them*?"

"Correct, ma'am; that is what is known as politics! What is especially cunning about this plan," the Prime Minister went on, unrolling a diagram, "is that we'll build the bridge from the top of our wall to the top of theirs and then lower ourselves down on ropes!"

"Did you say invade Aralia?" asked the King of Zedonia.
"Absolutely, your Majesty!" replied the Chancellor with
great enthusiasm. "And this we will do by means of a tunnel!
We simply dig down, beneath the walls, under the river and
come up in the middle of Aralia!"

The Queen of Aralia looked puzzled. "But how will the bridge be held up?"

"It's all rather technical," said the Prime Minister, referring to his diagram. "Pulleys, cantilevers, rods, poles, perches—that sort of thing . . ."

"I suppose you know what you're doing," sighed the Queen. "I must say it would be nice to have cream with my strawberries again."

"Unfortunately, ma'am, at the moment, there *aren't* any strawberries!"

The King of Zedonia scratched his head. "But how will you know when you're under the middle of Aralia?"

"Couldn't be simpler, your Majesty," said the Chancellor waving vaguely at a plan. "It's all a question of latitudes, longitudes, meantimes and meridians!"

"Then you'd better start digging," said the King. "I must say it would be nice to have strawberries with my cream again."

"You forget, your Majesty," snapped the Chancellor, "there *isn't* any cream!"

So the people of Aralia started building their bridge. They fixed up scaffolding, screwed brackets to the walls, tied ropes to towers and lowered planks from the battlements, until it reached across the valley to the walls of Zedonia.

Meanwhile the people of Zedonia started digging their
tunnel to Aralia. They burrowed this way and that, shovelling
and scratching and scraping at the earth until they decided
they were directly beneath Aralia.

One morning, several days later, the Queen of Aralia
climbed up to the top of the wall in order to try out the bridge.
At about the same time, the King of Zedonia got down on
his hands and knees and began to crawl into the long,
winding, dirty tunnel.

"This way, your Majesty," called the Chancellor. "Mind your head!"

"It's terribly—ouch!—dark in here!" said the King, stopping to rub his head. "How much further is it?"

"One more shovelful, your Majesty, and up we'll come in the middle of Aralia!"

One more shovelful, and up they came!

"This isn't the middle of Aralia!" shouted the King, feeling rather muddy. "This is the middle of the river!"

"Oh, but it can't be, your Majesty," answered the Chancellor, "rivers are wet!"

"Not during a drought, they're not!" bellowed the King. "We didn't need to dig a tunnel, we could have..." The King stopped short. There was a strange creaking noise. He looked up and saw the bridge swaying to and fro. There, wobbling along it, was the Queen of Aralia followed by the Prime Minister.

Suddenly there was a terrible snapping of ropes and a splintering of wood! The Queen of Aralia and her Prime Minister landed—PLOP!—in the mud right next to the King of Zedonia and his Chancellor.

When they got over their surprise, the King and Queen
asked each other what they were doing. Both said they were
on their way to ask the other for help. Sensibly, neither of
them mentioned the word "invade"!

"You know," said the Queen of Aralia, "we were stupid
to build those walls!"

"True," replied the King of Zedonia. "I can't even
remember why we built them!"

"*We* can!" interrupted the Prime Minister and the
Chancellor.

"Be quiet!" shouted the King of Zedonia.

"Yes," added the Queen of Aralia, "we've had enough of
your foolishness!"

SPLISH! Something very like a spot of rain fell out of the sky! SPLASH! Then came another spot! SPLOSH! And another! It began as a shower, but soon it was a torrential downpour.

The King and Queen looked at each other and smiled. They laughed and shook hands. Then they started dancing about in the rain, while the Chancellor and the Prime Minister looked on in horror.

"I've had an idea!" said the King of Zedonia.

"So have I!" said the Queen of Aralia.

"Let's knock these walls down!!" they both said together.

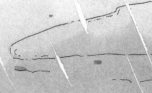

So the people of Aralia and Zedonia took picks and hammers and mallets and axes and crowbars and knocked down the two great walls. And with all the stones they built a fine new bridge across the river which was soon flowing through the valley once more.

When the bridge was finished, they built a stone archway at either end. But they didn't put up any gates, because they wanted to make sure the people were free to come and go as they pleased.

In Aralia, the plants and trees soon began to grow again.
In Zedonia, the cattle found lots of nice new grass to chew on.
Everything got back to normal.

Very soon, people started crossing the bridge from Aralia
with sweet green peas, dark purple plums, juicy yellow pears,
round white cauliflowers and baskets of strawberries for the
people of Zedonia.

And, on the way, they would pass people from Zedonia crossing the bridge with cool fresh milk, golden yellow butter, large brown eggs, mild crumbly cheese and jugs of thick cream for the people of Aralia.

And that is how the people of both towns managed to live happily ever after!

The inspiration for this story came from
GEOFF MARSHALL TAYLOR
who, long ago now, asked me to write a story
for schools radio, on the theme of barriers and bridges.
In turning that story into this one,
I was greatly helped by
DAVID WEEKS
who also thought up the subtitle,
A Little Give and Take,
which is really what it is all about.
This book is for them,
with affection and gratitude
from the Author.

Text copyright © 1994 Brian Sibley
Illustrations copyright © 1994 Rosslyn Moran

The author asserts the moral right
to be identified as the author of this work

Published by
Lion Publishing plc
Sandy Lane West, Oxford, England
ISBN 0 7459 2461 1
Lion Publishing
850 North Grove Avenue, Elgin, Illinois 60120, USA
ISBN 0 7459 2461 1
Albatross Books Pty Ltd
PO Box 320, Sutherland, NSW 2232, Australia
ISBN 0 7324 0827 X

First edition 1994

A catalogue record for this book is available
from the British Library

Library of Congress CIP Data applied for

Printed and bound in Malaysia